SO-ADZ-425

DUE DATE

OCT. 06.1994	MAY 21.1997	~~OCT.~~	
JAN. 25.1995	JUN. 13.1997		
MAR 15.1995	AUG. 22.1997		
OCT. 24.1995			
	FEB. 11.1998		
NOV. 25.1995	JUN. 02.1998		
	NOV 19.1993		
JAN. 19.1996	FEB 20.1999		
FEB. 22.1996	FEB. 04.2000		
APR. 05.1996			
	MAR 03.2000		
~~JUN. 13.1996~~			
FEB. 12.1997	JUL. 08.2000		
MAR 13.1999			
			Printed in USA

UNDER THE SUN AND THE MOON

MARGARET WISE BROWN
UNDER THE SUN
AND THE MOON
AND OTHER POEMS
Illustrated by TOM LEONARD

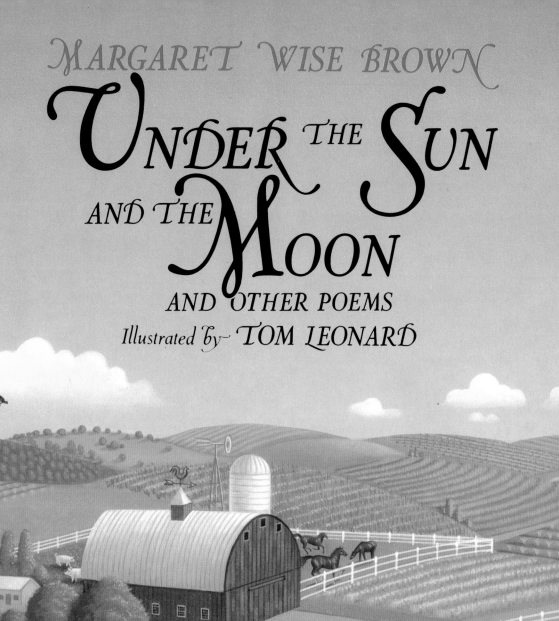

HYPERION BOOKS FOR CHILDREN
NEW YORK

CONTENTS

DREAM OF A WEED

Dream of a weed growing from a seed
Quietly, quietly from a seed
In a garden
A slim green weed
Quietly, quietly from a seed.

APPLE TREES

Apple trees as pink as pie
Like strawberry ice cream
In the sky
Burst on my
Delighted eye.

SONG OF LITTLE THINGS

Oh sing a song of little things
Of bugs and flies and flickering wings
Of flakes of snow and drops of rain
And yellow flowers in the lane
Of little pairs of squeaky shoes
And mice that laugh until they snooze
Of stars and pins and crumbs of cake
And bugs that laugh themselves awake.

From a Hornet's Nest

A swarm of hornets flew out from a hornet's nest
All on a summer's day.
Who to sting? Who to bite?
They buzzed and they buzzed and swarmed away
High in the sky where it was easy to fly
And look about with their hornet's eye
For anything for a hornet to sting
On foot or fin or feet or wing.
But this day they didn't see a thing
In wood or pond, in field or hay,
So they stung each other
And home they flew
All on a summer's day.

A COTTONTAIL RABBIT IN A COTTON FIELD

A cottontail rabbit in a cotton field
Jumped in the air and gave a squeal
His little tail flashed
White in the light
A cottontail flashing
In clear plain sight
But no one saw him in the cotton field
And only the cold wind heard him squeal.

NONSENSE SONG

A long way from Nowhere
In the Land of Nothing
Two pussycats sat in a tree.
How did they get there?
And where did they come from?
On that they could never agree.

Run, Bun, Run

Said a bun
To a bun,
"Why don't you run
Out in the grass
And have some fun?"

Said a bun
To a bun,
"I refuse to run
When I can sit
And dream in the sun."

Run, bun, run,
Or sit in the sun.
Sit in the sun,
Or run, bun, run.

10

MOUSE OF MY HEART

Mouse mouse
Why do you start
Timid and shy
As a human heart?

Mouse mouse
Where do you glide
Like a soft gray shadow
Trying to hide?

Mouse mouse
Where is your den
Far from the eyes
of cats and men?

THE TIGER'S CHILD

Ssssssssssssssspit
I'm Wild Cat Wild
The Tiger's child
I bristle my hairs
And scratch down chairs
And arch my back at terrible bears
I'm Wild Cat Wild
The Tiger's child
Ssssssssssssssspit.

SAID A BUG

Said a bug to a bug,
"Look away up high
At those great green grass blades
Piercing the sky."

Said a bug to a bug,
"How high is the sky
Above the grass blades,
Grass blades so high?"

Said the other bug,
"It depends on the eye
Of the bug that is looking
Up in the sky.
Some bugs crawl
And some bugs fly."

Said a bug to a bug,
"Buzz up and fly
Above those grass blades
Into the sky.
But
    don't
        bump
            into
                a
                    butterfly!"

16

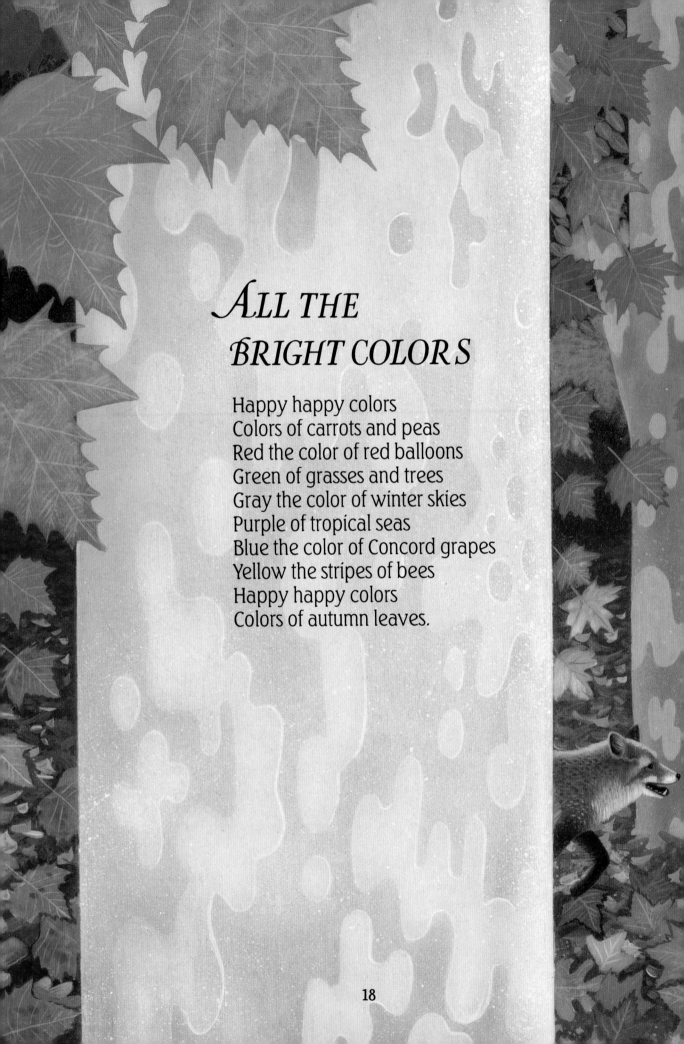

ALL THE BRIGHT COLORS

Happy happy colors
Colors of carrots and peas
Red the color of red balloons
Green of grasses and trees
Gray the color of winter skies
Purple of tropical seas
Blue the color of Concord grapes
Yellow the stripes of bees
Happy happy colors
Colors of autumn leaves.

I Dreamed of a Horse

I dreamed of a horse
A quiet horse
And the horse belonged to me

I dreamed of a horse
A great white horse
In a land beyond the sea

I dreamed of a horse
A golden horse
In the time of chivalry

I dreamed of a horse
A gentle horse
And the horse belonged to me.

GOLDEN AIR

When the wind blows
The leaves fall free
Yellow leaves falling
In golden air

And everywhere
Upon the ground
Leaves of gold
Are scattered round.

THE FARMER'S LULLABY

Silently the first star comes
The moon rides up the sky
The little mice scamper about in the hay
And the horses stomp and sigh
One last moo from a dreaming cow
And the old pig winks his eye
And the fireflies fly by
In the Farmer's Lullaby.

24

DROWSY LITTLE BUMBLEBEE

Drowsy little bumblebee
Come and rest your wings on me
No more humming in the sun
Stars come out and day is done.

TWO LITTLE RACCOONS

Two little raccoons in the moon's dim light
Sat in a tree and held on tight
While a dark bird sang
In the tender night,
"Spoon up the moon
Spoon up the moon
Spoon up the moon."

Three White Rabbits Running

There were three white rabbits running
There were three white rabbits running
There were three white rabbits running
And they ran far away
And they ran far away
And they ran far away
Little tracks across the white snow
Rabbit tracks across the soft snow
Little tracks across the white snow
And they ran far away
And they ran far away
And they ran far away.

UNDER THE SUN
AND THE MOON

Go to sleep my bunny
Oh go to sleep my bun
Under the sun and the moon
Go to sleep my bunny
Oh go to sleep my bun
You'll be a big rabbit soon

    Go to sleep my kitty
    Oh go to sleep my cat
    Under the sun and the moon
    Go to sleep my kitty
    Oh go to sleep my cat
    You'll be a tiger cat soon

Go to sleep my owlet
Oh go to sleep my owl
Under the sun and the moon
Go to sleep my owlet
Oh go to sleep my owl
And you'll be a hoot owl soon

Go to sleep my puppy
Oh go to sleep my dog
Under the sun and the moon
Go to sleep my puppy
Oh go to sleep my dog
And you'll be a sheepdog soon

Go to sleep my teddy
Oh go to sleep my bear
Under the sun and the moon
Go to sleep my teddy
Oh go to sleep my bear
And you'll be a big bear soon

Go to sleep my baby
Oh go to sleep my girl
Under the sun and the moon
Go to sleep my baby
Oh go to sleep my girl
You'll be a young lady soon

Go to sleep my baby
Oh go to sleep my boy
Under the sun and the moon
Go to sleep my baby
Oh go to sleep my boy
And you'll be a grown man soon.

FIRST EDITION
1 3 5 7 9 10 8 6 4 2

_____

Library of Congress Cataloging-in-Publication Data

Brown, Margaret Wise, 1910–1952.
Under the sun and the moon and other poems/by Margaret Wise
Brown; illustrated by Tom Leonard — 1st ed.
p.   cm.
Summary: A collection of previously unpublished poems, including
"Apple Trees," "From a Hornet's Nest," and "I Dreamed of a Horse."
ISBN 1-56282-354-X (trade) — ISBN 1-56282-355-8 (lib. bdg.)
1. Children's poetry, American.   [1. American poetry.]
I. Leonard, Thomas, 1955–   ill.   II. Title.
PS3503.R82184U53   1993
811'.52 — dc20   92-72031   CIP   AC